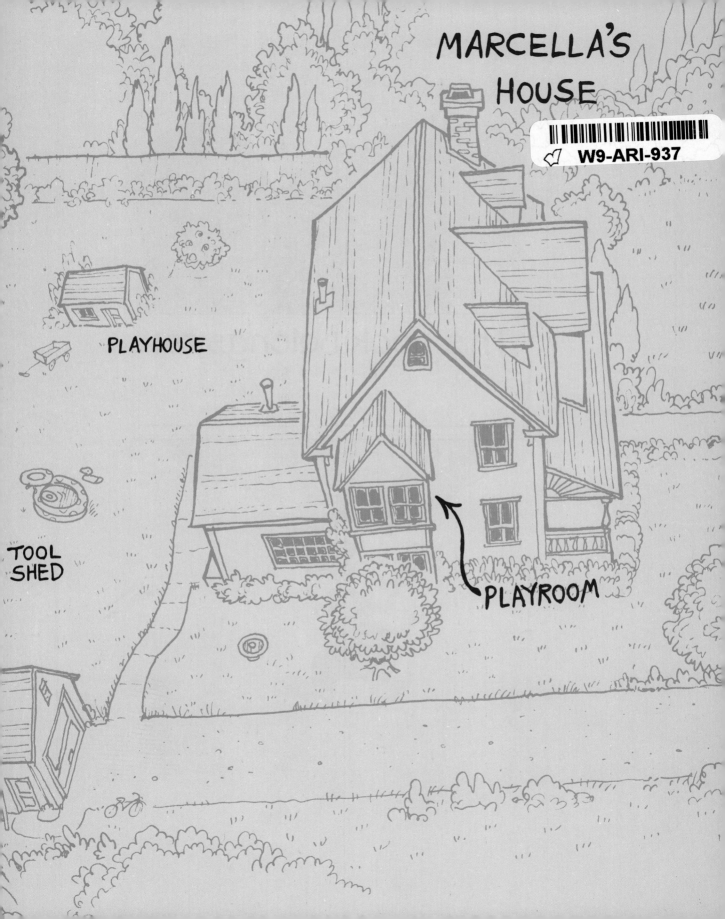

MARCELLA'S HOUSE

PLAYHOUSE

TOOL SHED

PLAYROOM

This book belongs to:

Merry Christmas from Uncle Tom +
Aunt Dawn

Sarah Woelke

Raggedy Ann & Andy's

RAGGEDY DOG LEARNS TO SHARE

A LYNX BOOK

This book is published by Lynx Books, a division of Lynx Communications, Inc., 41 Madison Avenue, New York, New York 10010. The name "Lynx" together with the logotype consisting of a stylized head of a lynx is a trademark of Lynx Communications, Inc.

Raggedy Ann and Andy's Grow-and-Learn Library, the names and depictions of Raggedy Ann, Raggedy Andy and all related characters are trademarks of Macmillan, Inc.

It was a very rainy morning, so Marcella decided to play ball with Fido in the playroom.

"Here, Fido, catch this!" Marcella called. "Here it comes! Catch the ball. Good boy!"

Raggedy Dog loved to watch the ball fly through the air. He loved to watch Fido jump up high and catch it every time. When Fido was around, Raggedy Dog never noticed anyone else—not even Marcella.

Then the ball rolled very fast across the floor—right under Raggedy Dog's nose! Fido chased it, and when he came to Raggedy Dog, he looked right into Raggedy Dog's eyes. Fido could see how much Raggedy Dog wanted to play with the ball. But Fido couldn't play with him while Marcella was in the playroom.

Just then Marcella looked out the window.
"Oh, Fido, look. It's stopped raining," she said. "Let's
go outside now." And Marcella ran toward the door.

As Marcella left the playroom, Fido followed her. But to Raggedy Dog's surprise, Fido didn't take the ball. Fido dropped the ball and rolled it right to the place where Raggedy Dog was sitting.

"Have fun," barked Fido, and with a wag of his tail, he
bounded quickly down the stairs.

With a leap, Raggedy Dog pounced on the ball. He was so happy to have a chance to play with Fido's special ball! He wanted to run and jump and catch that ball—just like Fido.

"Look, everyone," called Raggedy Andy. "Raggedy Dog has Fido's ball!"

"Let's play catch," suggested Sunny Bunny.
"Great idea," agreed Tim the Toy Soldier.
"Let go of the ball, Raggedy Dog," said Greta the
Dutch Doll. "Then we can all play."

"Oh, no," barked Raggedy Dog, and he held the ball away from them all.

Playing ball with the other dolls wasn't what Raggedy Dog had in mind. He wanted to run and jump and catch the ball all by himself, just like Fido. Besides, Fido had given the ball to him—not to Raggedy Andy or Greta or Tim or Sunny Bunny.

Raggedy Andy reached for the ball. Raggedy Dog had it firmly beneath his paws.

"Aren't you going to share?" Raggedy Andy asked him.

Sharing was the one thing Raggedy Dog was *not* going to do.

Just then Raggedy Ann walked over.
"What's wrong?" she asked, and the dolls all told her
what had happened.

"Never mind," she said to the others. "We'll play something else now. Maybe Raggedy Dog will want to share the ball later." And Raggedy Ann and Raggedy Andy and Greta and Sunny Bunny and all of the other dolls went to the other side of the playroom to play.

At last Raggedy Dog had Fido's special ball all to himself. And Raggedy Dog began to play with it just like Fido. First he danced around the ball, waiting for it to fly across the room. He wanted to run and jump and catch it as it sailed through the air. But the ball just sat there. It did not move.

"Come on, ball, fly," urged Raggedy Dog. He picked up the ball and spun around and around. Then he threw the ball as hard as he could.

But Raggedy Dog couldn't throw the ball very high or very far. And he couldn't catch it as it flew through the air.

Raggedy Dog remembered how much fun Fido had when he chased the ball as it rolled across the floor.

"I'll try that," he thought hopefully.

So Raggedy Dog took his paw and pushed the ball.

But it hardly budged. It didn't roll fast, and it didn't roll far.

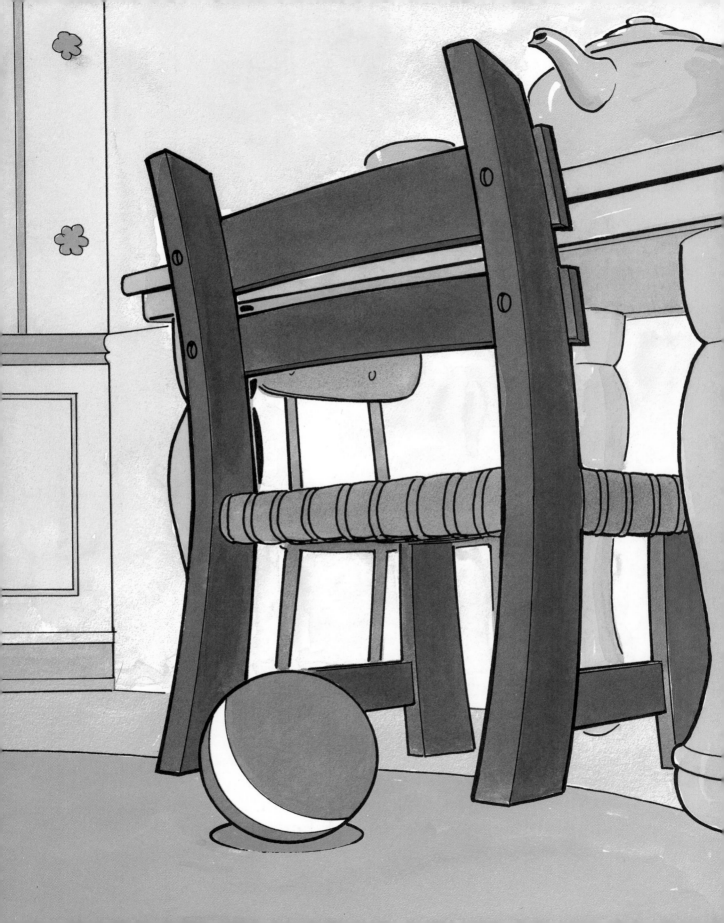

Raggedy Dog just didn't understand. Fido's special ball wasn't much fun after all. It was fun for Fido, but not for him. And Raggedy Dog couldn't figure out why.

"Maybe Fido's ball only works for Fido," Raggedy Dog thought to himself. "Well, if that's the way it wants to be, I don't want to play with it anyway." Then he turned his back on the ball, and he sat with his head on his paws and pouted.

Just then The Camel with the Wrinkled Knees woke up from his nap and walked over to Raggedy Dog.

"What's wrong?" he asked. He didn't know anything about what had happened with Fido's ball.

"It's this ball," Raggedy Dog barked. "Fido gave it to me. But it isn't any fun. It won't fly through the air or roll fast on the ground. It only works for Fido."

"Well, I don't know much about playing ball," The Camel with the Wrinkled Knees said slowly. "But I think it's the kind of thing that's hard to do alone."

"But Fido can . . . " Raggedy Dog started to say. Then he thought for a moment. At last he figured it out.

Something was missing from the game—and now he knew just what it was. He needed someone to share the ball with, the way Fido did with Marcella!

Raggedy Dog picked up the ball and ran right over to the other side of the playroom where all his friends were.

"Want to play ball?" barked Raggedy Dog, wagging his tail very hard.

"Oh, hi, Raggedy Dog," said Raggedy Andy in a not-very-friendly voice.

"We're having fun without Fido's ball," added Sunny Bunny.

"We're very busy right now," said Greta.

Raggedy Dog stopped wagging his tail. He didn't understand. Why didn't his friends want to play with him and the ball now? That was all they had wanted to do just a short time ago. Confused, Raggedy Dog walked over to Raggedy Ann. He put down the ball and sat beside her.

"Why don't they want to play ball with me?" Raggedy Dog asked her.

"Maybe you hurt their feelings when you wouldn't share with them," Raggedy Ann suggested.

"I guess I didn't think very much about what anyone else wanted to do," Raggedy Dog agreed. "But we could have fun now," he added softly, "if anyone wanted to play."

"Come," said Raggedy Ann. "I'll throw the ball to you." So Raggedy Ann and Raggedy Dog started to play ball.

Before long, Raggedy Andy joined in . . .

and then Tim and Greta and Sunny Bunny, too.
They all played with Fido's special ball.

Now the ball flew through the air.
And it rolled across the floor.

Each doll caught the ball and, in turn, threw it to the next doll.

When the dolls ended their game, Raggedy Dog said, "I'm sorry!" He told his friends, "I thought it would be more fun to have the ball all to myself. But it's much more fun to play with you!"

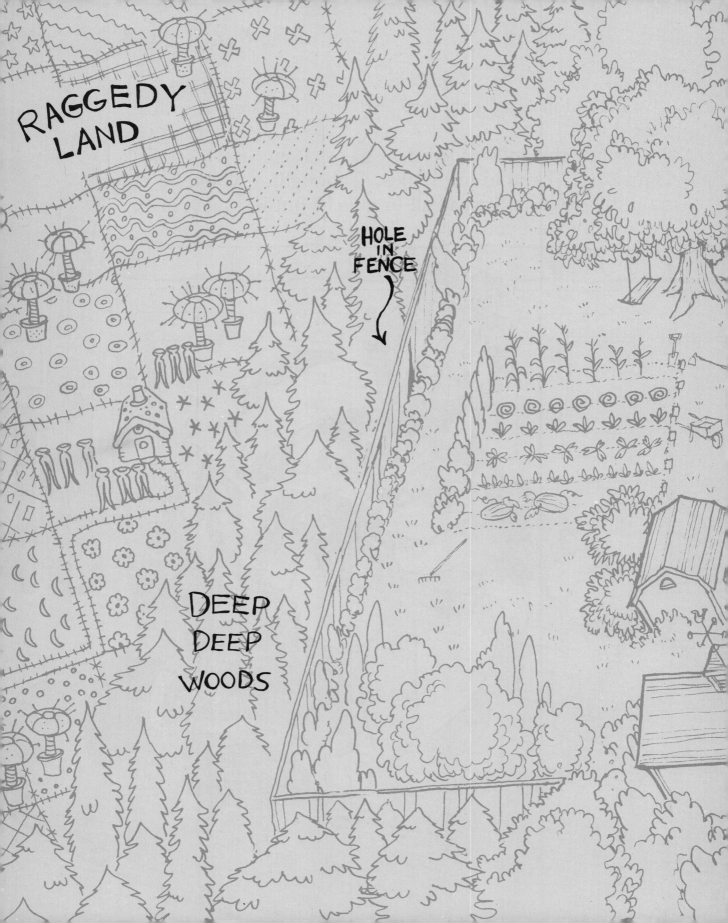